Can you read to me?

CLAIRE'S BOOKS

36

Of course! But first we have to find...

THE PERFECT SEAT

𝒟ISNEP • HYPERION   LOS ANGELES   NEW YORK

BY
MINH LÊ
&
GUS GORDON

502

This side for the Address.

Too Big.

Too Small.

Too Old.

Too New.

Too Rough.

Too Slippery.

Should the perfect seat
make you this dizzy?

Too Thin.

Too

Wide.

Too Tall.

Too Short.

Too Funky.

What about here?

Are you okay down there ?

Oh, I give up.

FOUND IT !

PERFECT.

For Jacob and Ezra, who make every story time perfect.
—M.L.

For Rob. A dedicated grandad.
—G.G.

Text copyright © 2019 by Minh Lê
Illustrations copyright © 2019 by Gus Gordon

First Edition, November 2019
10 9 8 7 6 5 4 3 2 1
FAC-029191-19270
Printed in Malaysia

This book is hand-lettered, with copyright and flaps set in Mrs Eaves/Fontspring
Designed by Jamie Alloy
The illustrations were created using watercolors, pencils, crayon, and collage.

Library of Congress Cataloging-in-Publication Data

Names: Le, Minh, 1979- author. • Gordon, Gus, illustrator. • Title: The perfect seat / by Minh Le ; pictures by Gus Gordon. • Description: First edition. • Los Angeles ; New York : Disney-Hyperion, 2019. • Summary: Eager to read together, a parent and child search for the perfect seat. • Identifiers: LCCN 2018061310• ISBN 9781368020046 (hardcover) • ISBN 1368020046 (hardcover) • Subjects: • CYAC: Chairs—Fiction. • Books and reading—Fiction. • Parent and child—Fiction. • Classification: LCC PZ7.1.L39 Per 2019 • DDC [E]—dc23 LC record available at https://lccn.loc.gov/2018061310

Reinforced binding

Visit www.DisneyBooks.com